The Jacksons

by
Cass R. Sandak

CRESTWOOD HOUSE
New York

Maxwell Macmillan Canada
Toronto

Maxwell Macmillan International
New York Oxford Singapore Sydney

Library of Congress Cataloging-in-Publication Data
Sandak, Cass R.
The Jacksons / by Cass R. Sandak. — 1st ed.
p. cm. — (First families)
Includes bibliographical references and index.
Summary: An account of the life of Andrew Jackson and his family with an emphasis on his years as president.
ISBN 0-89686-636-X
1. Jackson, Andrew, 1767–1845—Juvenile literature. 2. Jackson, Rachel, 1767–1828—Juvenile literature. 3. Presidents—United States—Biography—Juvenile literature. 4. Presidents—United States—Wives—Biography—Juvenile literature. 5. Jackson family—Juvenile literature. [1. Jackson, Andrew, 1767–1845. 2. Jackson, Rachel, 1767–1828. 3. Presidents. 4. First ladies.] I. Title. II. Series: Sandak, Cass R. First families.
E382.S26 1992
973.5'6'092—dc20
[B] 91-30363
CIP
AC

Photo Credits
Cover: The Hermitage—Home of Andrew Jackson
The Bettmann Archive: 4, 7, 9, 10, 13, 14, 17, 19, 20, 22, 25, 27, 29, 30, 32, 33, 35, 36, 39, 40, 41, 43, 44
The New York Public Library Picture Collection: 31, 42

CRESTWOOD HOUSE

Macmillan Publishing Company
866 Third Avenue
New York, NY 10022

Maxwell Macmillan Canada, Inc.
1200 Eglinton Avenue East
Suite 200
Don Mills, Ontario M3C 3N1

Macmillan Publishing Company is part of the Maxwell Communication Group of Companies.

Produced by Flying Fish Studio

Printed in the United States of America

First edition

10 9 8 7 6 5 4 3 2 1

Contents

A New Kind of Inauguration

The date was March 4, 1829. It was the day of the new president's inauguration. Andrew Jackson had given his speech, taken his oath of office and bowed low on the east portico of the Capitol building. When Jackson headed back to the White House, the crowd seemed to take it as a signal. A swarm of people began to storm the president's home. They all wanted to catch a glimpse of the new president.

Suddenly the president's home had become the people's. The reception following the inauguration ceremony had turned into an open house. No one had an invitation. Anyone who could squeeze in was eligible to meet the new president. Those in charge had expected a few hundred people. According to some sources, as many as 20,000 people showed up.

They came from all parts of the country and from all kinds of backgrounds. Men were seen sporting pistols in their belts. Some women wore necklaces of hickory nuts as a sign of support for Old Hickory. Elegant carriages parked next to humble farm carts. People in the finest silk clothing walked beside people in homespun garments. They all wanted to shake Andrew Jackson's hand.

A painting of the scene outside the White House after the inauguration of President Andrew Jackson.

Inside the White House, people stood on furniture so they could see better. As a result, a great deal of damage was done. Fistfights broke out, and shoving was one way of trying to get a better view. Because there were so many people, food and drink ran out very quickly. Large supplies of ice cream, cake and punch were exhausted within minutes.

Servants took refreshments out to the lawn in hopes of luring the crowd from the house. Glassware and china worth thousands of dollars were shattered. Men pulled out knives to hack off pieces of carpet or drapery to take home as souvenirs.

It was a new kind of presidency. Many people frowned on this kind of uncontrolled festivity. But it somehow made sense: If Jackson was one of the people, then surely he would welcome *them* when they wanted to see him. Like so many presidents, Jackson was a man of contradictions. Although he seemed a simple person, he was in fact extremely wealthy.

Despite all the merrymaking, for President Jackson himself a pall of sadness hung over the day. Jackson's beloved wife, Rachel, had died after the election, just before Christmas. She was not around to share in this great moment of joy and triumph for Jackson.

There is some indication that Mrs. Jackson died of a heart attack. But others think she may have died from a broken heart. A simple, stout woman, at age 61 Mrs. Jackson had heard some unkind gossip that said she was common. Some even suggested that Mrs. Jackson smoked

Portrait of Andrew Jackson

a pipe. In any event, Rachel Jackson had had little education and wrote with some difficulty.

Mrs. Jackson had been planning to move with her husband into the White House. But shortly before Christmas she weakened and sensed she was going to die. Mrs. Jackson's nephew's wife, Emily Donelson, was asked to serve as the official White House hostess. Mrs. Jackson had never really taken to Washington nor had society in the nation's capital thought highly of her. She had once said, "I had rather be a doorkeeper in the House of God than live in that palace in Washington."

President Jackson missed his wife intensely in the midst of the noise and excitement. On this Inauguration Day, the crowd quickly got out of hand. People pressed through the entire White House, damaging anything they could get their hands on. Aides feared for the president's safety and whisked Jackson away from the mansion to a small hotel nearby.

Jackson saw himself as an ordinary person. By opening up the White House doors to all visitors he linked himself with his fellow Americans. No one before had had the same kind of appeal. But forever after, the view of the president as "one of the boys" would be a common one.

The Young Jackson

Jackson's parents were Andrew and Elizabeth Hutchinson Jackson. They had both come to the United States from northern Ireland in 1765. They landed on the East Coast and then moved south and settled in the Waxhaw region, between North and South Carolina. Because no one is certain to which state the land belonged, both North Carolina and South Carolina claim Jackson was born there! Jackson, however, always said his birthplace was in South Carolina.

The Jacksons had two older sons who had been born when the family still lived in Ireland. Jackson's father died suddenly early in 1767. Shortly after his death, Mrs. Jackson gave birth to her third son on March 15, 1767. He was named Andrew after his late father.

Legend says that Andrew Jackson was the first president who had been born in a log cabin. No one knows for sure. Even Jackson himself wasn't clear on this point. But it makes a good story.

Soon after her husband died, Mrs. Jackson and her sons moved into a nearby house to live with Jane Crawford and her family. Mrs. Crawford was Mrs. Jackson's sister.

Mrs. Jackson was a serious and devout woman. More than anything, she wanted her son Andrew to become a Presbyterian minister. But this kind of life was not what Andrew had in mind. When he was about 12 or 13, young Andrew left school. He spent some time drifting, uncertain about himself and his future.

Jackson was just 13 when he became a follower of a local militia group. The group's aim was to drive the British from their part of South Carolina. Young Andrew was taken prisoner by the British, who mistreated him.

In 1780, some British soldiers staged the Waxhaw Massacre. It was an unexpected raid, and more than 100 of the local people were killed. The event made Andrew hate the British strongly. Around the same time a British soldier asked Andrew to polish his boots. Andrew refused, but the incident added to his hatred of the British. His mother had come from Ireland, where some people hated the British. This may also have instilled in Andrew his strong dislike of the English.

Young Andrew Jackson at the Waxhaw Massacre

Whatever the reasons, by the time he was barely a teenager, Andrew knew that he did not want to have anything to do with the British. Being part of the United States—a new country free of British control—was what mattered.

It was also during the period following the Waxhaw Massacre that Jackson's older brothers died. And Mrs. Jackson fell ill while tending to British prisoners. She died of fever a short time later. By the time he was 14, Andrew was an orphan.

Famous oil painting of President Andrew Jackson

From this time forward Andrew Jackson had to make his own way in the world. He learned to be tough and self-sufficient. There were those who thought Andrew had a bad temper. They wanted to stay on his good side. There were always stories about Andrew's youthful gambling, his horse racing and his hard drinking.

About 1783 Jackson may have received a modest inheritance from his paternal grandfather, Hugh Jackson. It appears that the money was spent quickly on cards and at races and also to pay off gambling debts.

In 1784 Jackson must have begun to think about the future. He moved to Salisbury, North Carolina. There he began to study law. In those days young lawyers "read" law and worked in attorneys' offices. They didn't go to law school, as people do today. Jackson worked for about 2 1/2 years in two different law offices. Then he was examined by judges and deemed qualified to begin his legal practice.

Jackson was largely uneducated. He was outspoken and more interested in fighting than in reading books. Even though he was a lawyer, he was ill spoken and his spelling was poor. An enemy said of Jackson, "His letters with their crudities in spelling and grammar, would make the better educated angels weep."

When Jackson finished his studies in 1787, he was licensed to practice law in North Carolina. He moved to the extreme western end of the state, to an area that would later become part of Tennessee. This marked his introduction to the state of Tennessee and the city of Nashville, which would become his home for the rest of his life.

Jackson in Nashville

Jackson first arrived in Nashville in 1788. By this time he was 21 years old. Jackson had a forceful, commanding presence. He stood over six feet tall. He was extremely slender, weighing only about 150 pounds. He had thick, dark hair—although it began to turn gray at an early age—and penetrating blue eyes. Many people who knew him recalled that Andrew Jackson smoked a long-stemmed clay pipe much of the time.

Soon after arriving in Nashville, Andrew Jackson became a popular figure in and around the city. He moved into a boardinghouse run by a Mrs. Donelson. During this time he first met Rachel Donelson Robards, the woman he would marry.

Within a short time the young lawyer was handling half of the pending court cases in Nashville. Often his clients lacked the money to pay his fees, so they gave him slaves and land in payment for his services. He also made good friends who would help him later in his political life. He was quickly able to accumulate 600 acres of land near Nashville, which would eventually become his plantation, the Hermitage. During this time Jackson was becoming a fairly wealthy man.

In 1791, Jackson became an attorney general for a district around Nashville. He also returned to military life. In the same year Jackson became a judge associated with a local militia group.

By 1796 Tennessee had become a state, and Jackson served as Tennessee's first representative in the U.S. House

As a young lawyer, Andrew Jackson tries a case before a judge in New Orleans.

of Representatives. Then he became a U.S. senator and had to go to Philadelphia, which was then the nation's capital. But he served only one session, about five months. He was homesick away from Tennessee and missed his family. In 1798, Jackson was appointed a judge of the Superior Court of Tennessee. He served in this capacity for six years.

A vital and energetic man, Jackson led an active life. To add to his income Jackson ran a general store. On a piece of land next to the Hermitage he ran a racetrack. He also became a major general of the Tennessee militia.

Rachel Donelson Jackson

Rachel Donelson Jackson

The woman Andrew Jackson married had been born in Virginia in 1767. It was the same year Andrew Jackson had been born. One of eleven children, Rachel Donelson came to Tennessee with her family when she was only 12. By the time she was 17 she had married a man named Lewis Robards.

Rachel was still a sweet-faced, black-haired beauty when she met Jackson. Rachel's father was retired army colonel John Donelson. When her father died, the family took in boarders.

When Jackson arrived in Nashville in 1788, he rented rooms in a house belonging to the colonel's widow. The home was like a boardinghouse, where Jackson paid for his lodgings and meals. The Donelsons' daughter Rachel lived there with her husband. Lewis turned out to be lazy and shiftless. Although they separated several times during the course of their short marriage, the couple was making another attempt to reconcile.

As fate would have it, soon after Jackson met Rachel he fell in love with her. Most people seem to feel that Jackson did not break up the Robardses' marriage. Firm evidence exists that the marriage was already an unhappy one long before Rachel and Andrew met.

Eventually Jackson married Rachel Donelson Robards not once, but twice. The first time was in 1791 in Natchez, Mississippi. Neither of them knew at this time that her first marriage was not legally over. It seems to have been a completely innocent error. Rachel was under the impression that her husband had applied for and been granted a divorce. But in fact, he had merely received permission to file for one. It wasn't until 1793 that the divorce decree was official. Rachel and Andrew Jackson remarried in January of 1794. This time it was a quiet ceremony conducted in Nashville. At the time there was gossip that Jackson had run off with a married woman. When he campaigned for the presidency the gossip turned nasty.

Despite his popularity, Jackson did have a number of political enemies. These people spread slanderous words both about Rachel and about her second marriage. Because Andrew was devoted to Rachel, he was always quick and eager to defend his wife's honor. Jackson was also, by most accounts, a hot-tempered man. Some estimates show that Jackson may have been involved in over 100 duels during his lifetime.

In 1806, Jackson took part in a duel that nearly ended his life. A man named Charles Dickinson had upset Jackson, most likely because he had insulted Rachel. A bullet from Dickinson's gun lodged in Jackson's chest next to his heart. Because the bullet was in such a dangerous place, it could never be removed. Jackson carried it with him until the end of his life.

Dickinson died as a result of the duel. Although Jackson was never put on trial, Dickinson's death was one of the events that made people think of Jackson a little more cautiously.

Jackson was involved in another famous duel in 1813. This time, Jackson was not the principal in the duel, but the backup, or second. But the principal's brother was outraged that Jackson was involved even as a second. The brother then challenged Jackson himself to a duel.

A Devoted Couple

Rachel Donelson Jackson was neither a loose woman nor a saint. The truth lay somewhere in the middle. At worst, Rachel was probably a flirt. At least one person

described Rachel as unduly pious. Whatever the truth, the two made a fine couple, deeply devoted to one another. Their marriage lasted nearly 40 years until Rachel's death.

As guests in society, the Jacksons were not precisely in demand. The scandal of divorce did not fully explain their unpopularity as a couple. Probably no one cared whether or not the Jacksons were legally wed for the first two years of their marriage—except strong political enemies. The things that kept Mrs. Jackson from being popular were her lack of polish and education. Even in the early days of the country, Washington society was beginning to take itself seriously. But Rachel Jackson cared nothing for fine things or sophistication. She was over 50 before she left Tennessee, and she did not find Washington to her liking.

Despite all this, the Jacksons were seemingly happy with one another. After Rachel's death, Jackson remained completely devoted to her memory. It is said that he carried around a miniature portrait of Rachel during his waking hours. And at night as he slept the portrait stayed on his bedside table.

Rachel was unpretentious and kind. Surviving portraits show a sensitive woman with an intelligent face. She was attractive, although as she grew older she became increasingly heavy. She was a warm and welcoming hostess and endeared herself to many who knew her.

The Jacksons had no children of their own. In fact, Andrew Jackson had no close blood relatives. The Jacksons did have an adopted son, Andrew Jackson, Jr. He was the son of Rachel's brother, and the Jacksons adopted him when he was only four days old. Rachel Jackson had an-

The young Emily Donelson, Jackson's first official hostess at the White House

other nephew named Andrew Jackson Donelson. The couple regarded him almost as a son. Andrew Donelson married his cousin Emily. Because Rachel died before Jackson became president, Emily Donelson served as official hostess at the White House. When Jackson was inaugurated, Emily was only 21. She and her husband had four children, three of whom were born while the family was living in the White House.

But Emily herself was not a strong person and died of tuberculosis in 1836. Jackson had only a few months left to serve of his second term. During this time, Sarah Yorke Jackson, Andrew Jackson, Jr.'s wife, took over the White House duties. It was Sarah who then stayed with the president and became his companion and nurse for the rest of his life.

The Creek War

Andrew Jackson became famous through his military successes. Jackson was not a brilliant soldier. He was certainly not a military strategist. But he was a strong and determined leader. He had been a youngster during the Revolutionary War. But as an adult he found himself embroiled in the War of 1812. This war was an aftermath of the Revolution. The British still seemed to hold a grudge against

Creek chief surrendering to Andrew Jackson at the end of the Creek War

their former colonists. In addition, many Indians felt that American settlers were anxious to open up the lands to the west. This meant that the Americans would remove the Indians, by force if necessary, to keep the land available for settlement. One Shawnee leader, Tecumseh, was particularly anxious to keep his land for his tribe. The British therefore allied themselves with the Indians against the Americans. This was one of the major issues of the war.

In 1813 the Creek Indians attacked the white settlers at Fort Mims in the Mississippi Territory. The Creeks had joined forces with Tecumseh on the side of the British. More than 400 people were killed in this uprising.

Jackson led a group of volunteers to retaliate against the Creek Indians. For five months Jackson and the Creeks fought against each other's forces. Then, in 1814, in a bloody battle, 900 Indians were killed at Horseshoe Bend. At a fort there the military leader negotiated a treaty. The fort was named Fort Jackson and the document that ended the fighting was known as the Treaty of Fort Jackson.

Nine months of war were over. A larger surrender than the tribe's was at stake, though. When the Creeks gave up to Jackson, they also gave up some 20 million acres of land that included most of Alabama and some of Georgia. The surrender meant that a huge parcel of land was now open for the westward expansion of the United States.

It was during this time that Jackson's men came to call him Old Hickory, to signify his toughness. He was loyal to those who served him. The nickname stuck and Jackson was known by it for the rest of his life.

Andrew Jackson (extreme right, on a white horse) *during the War of 1812*

The Battle of New Orleans

The Battle of New Orleans began in 1814, *after* the Treaty of Ghent had officially ended the War of 1812. The treaty was signed in Belgium at the end of 1814, but there was no telegraph in those days. It took a long time for messages to get from one side of the world to the other.

The war had been fought between the British and the Americans. The British were still camped along the Mississippi not far from New Orleans. In the Battle of New Orleans the Americans triumphed. It was a major battle in the war as well as the first great American military victory.

About five miles from New Orleans Jackson and his men built a wall. The American troops stayed behind this line, waiting. The technique worked and the British were lured into warfare. On January 8, 1815, the British decided to attack. But the battle lasted only about half an hour and was a rout for the British. Some 3,000 British soldiers were wounded or killed, while the American casualties were very light.

The country had fought hard only a few years before for independence. Now the victory at New Orleans made the military forces of the new country look even better. The struggle for independence had been worth the fight.

The Battle of New Orleans catapulted Andrew Jackson to fame. The frontier lawyer was now known as a great military leader. As a result of his victory, Jackson became well known, well liked and very much a popular favorite. From this time on, Jackson's becoming president seemed like a real possibility.

Congress even authorized a gold medal in 1815 to celebrate Jackson's success. Because of Jackson's popularity after the war, distinguished portrait painters, including Charles Willson Peale and Thomas Sully, were eager to paint his likeness. At first, Jackson was usually shown dressed in his military uniform. As he began to realize his potential as a politician, he sat for more and more artists in the civilian clothes of a national leader.

The Battle of New Orleans was the turning point in Andrew Jackson's life. From that moment on, he was admired across the nation. The victory gave him the push that was needed to turn a strong military figure into a candidate for the presidency. But he still wasn't quite ready for the job.

The Seminole War

In 1818 President James Monroe sent Jackson to punish the Seminole Indians. The Spaniards, who controlled Florida, and the Seminoles had banded together to keep outsiders from coming to live in the area. The U.S. government also learned that the Spanish were allowing runaway slaves to settle in the territory. Slavery was still legal in the southern United States at this time. The Seminole war that grew out of this situation stopped further Indian uprisings and drove away the Spanish.

Jackson ordered two British civilians, Robert Ambrister and Alexander Arbuthnot, executed. The British protested and Congress was forced to ask about Jackson's behavior during the war. It would not be the first or last time that a deed of Jackson's would be questioned. But he seemed able to get away with most things.

After the brief Seminole war, President Monroe claimed that the United States had legally taken over Florida. But the British and the Spanish objected strongly to this conclusion, and Monroe was forced to rethink his position. He had miscalculated and had to withdraw. His change in position was almost academic, because just a year later the Spanish sold Florida to the United States. Now the transfer of land was legal and complete. And for a brief period, beginning in 1821, President Monroe made Andrew Jackson governor of Florida.

Jackson's election to the U.S. Senate in 1823–1824 was well planned. It was a calculated move in Jackson's strategy to become president.

The 1824 Election

In the 1824 presidential election Andrew Jackson suffered one of the strangest and most bitter defeats in American history. He won both the popular vote and the largest number of votes in the electoral college. Still, the election did not give Jackson a clear majority. Since the Constitution requires a majority, a runoff vote was held in Congress. The election had been among three strong contenders: John Quincy Adams, Henry Clay and Jackson. Clay lobbied his supporters to cast their new votes for Adams. In this way, John Quincy Adams won, becoming the choice as the country's sixth president.

The final election results were a great blow to Jackson. Although disappointed, Jackson tried not to show it. He began to plan how he would win in 1828. Jackson was nothing if not determined.

A political cartoon of Henry Clay sewing up Andrew Jackson's mouth.

He joined a group calculated to help him win. It was a newly formed political organization that we know today as the Democratic party. In the next election Jackson won an enormous victory. He ended up serving as president for two terms, from 1829 to 1837.

As a result of the election, there was very little good feeling between Jackson and Adams. Although Adams was a competent president, enough people remembered Jackson's close and largely undeserved defeat in 1824. And when election time rolled around again in 1828, there was little doubt who would be the next president. It was almost a certainty that Adams could not run again and win.

The 1828 Election

The 1828 election was one of the most eagerly anticipated events in American history. In that election three times as many people cast votes as in the 1824 election. The number of qualified voters had increased enormously since property ownership was no longer a requirement for voting in many states.

Before 1824 the electoral college had been the sole method of selecting the president. And the electors had all been appointed. Beginning with the 1828 election, members of the electoral college were voted into their positions. This more truly reflected the public's wishes. And so Jackson was the first president to gain office by a true popular vote.

All of the six previous presidents had come from Virginia or Massachusetts, but Jackson had been born on the frontier of the new United States. Jackson was the first

A full-length painting of Andrew Jackson

president who had not been born into the ranks of the privileged and wealthy. When Andrew Jackson became president it showed democracy at work. Many people became convinced that anyone could be president. You could be an ordinary person and still aspire to the nation's highest office.

Jackson's election was unique in other ways. For the first time, election handbills, banners, political slogans and rallies were part of the election process. Previous elections had been tastefully run. But not this one. In fact, it became very ugly, a mudslinging spectacle. The words "bigamist" and "adultery" directed against Jackson actually appeared on handbills. These were references to Rachel Jackson and the uncertain resolution of her first marriage and divorce. These words terrified Rachel and infuriated her husband.

Many of the insults came from John Quincy Adams's supporters. He represented an older, more refined political and social tradition. It is hard to believe that the Adams camp would be responsible for such ugly words, but indeed they were.

The final blow to Jackson came when Rachel Jackson died on December 22, 1828, weeks before she was to become first lady. Although it was a position she never had aspired to, there had been several insulting remarks made about her during the campaign. Many people said her spirit had been broken by the ugly gossip.

Although Washington society was never thrilled with Rachel Jackson, she was beloved in Tennessee. Most people in Nashville thought kindly of Rachel. Some 10,000 people turned up for her funeral, when the woman many locals called Aunt Rachel was laid to rest.

Rachel Jackson was quietly buried on Christmas Eve 1828 on the grounds of the Hermitage. Legend tells us she was wearing an elegant white gown. It was a dress that Rachel had chosen for her husband's inauguration, the event she never lived to see.

Rachel's death and Jackson's age (61) when he became president made him seem like an old man. Devoted to Rachel, he had been shattered by her death.

Jackson as President

Jackson was the first westerner to be president, and he was the first man of simple tastes.

Political cartooning first flourished with Andrew Jackson. He was a man of contradictory tastes and humble background and was a prime candidate for satire. Many people thought Jackson was too strong a leader as president. Some people ridiculed him by giving him the nickname "King Andrew the First." Artists drew pictures of him trampling the U.S. Constitution.

"King Andrew the First." A political cartoon of President Jackson as a dictator.

One of Jackson's first actions was to get rid of some 2,000 government officials. He dismissed them from their offices to make room for appointees of his own. Many of these people were friends of long standing, and it was Jackson's way of rewarding them. Some were even relatives. This was known as the "spoils" system. It came from the saying "To the victor belong the spoils."

Cartoon satirizing the "spoils" system

"The rats are leaving the falling house," cried the opposition when Andrew Jackson reorganized his cabinet. This is one of the many cartoons appearing throughout Jackson's presidency.

The term "kitchen cabinet" was first used during Jackson's presidency. Members of the cabinet would leave Jackson's office on the second floor of the White House through the kitchen. In this way they would not be seen. Eventually the expression came to mean that Jackson's cabinet was a bunch of cronies. The implication was that he was giving jobs to friends and relatives. To us, today, there is nothing surprising about this. But 150 years ago the idea was new and potentially dangerous.

Jackson was a strong leader who firmly believed in unity for the nation. Jackson grasped what the word "united" meant. He saw the strengths of self-government and believed strongly in the solidarity of the Union.

This principle was tested in 1832 when South Carolina wanted to leave the Union over certain states' rights issues. On December 10 Jackson drew up a proclamation asking the state to reconsider. The state leaders did, and the country was held together—at least temporarily—for another 30 years. Jackson's proclamation was one of his most significant achievements.

On January 30, 1835, an attempt was made on Jackson's life. The president was attending a funeral service in the Capitol rotunda in Washington. The service was for a representative who had recently died. From the crowd a gunman pulled out his weapon. But the bullets were damp and the gun didn't fire. A second gun also failed. The assailant was then taken into custody. A later trial proved the man unstable. It was the very first attempt made on a president's life. Sadly, it would not be the last.

A gunman attempts to kill President Jackson as he leaves the Capitol.

Lithographic cartoon of Andrew Jackson and the downfall of the Bank of the United States.

A Second Term

Henry Clay and Daniel Webster were strongly against Jackson, primarily because he wanted to be too strong a president. They were afraid Jackson would not defer to Congress and felt he should not misuse the presidential veto power. During his eight years as president, Jackson exercised his veto power twelve times. This was in contrast to the six presidents who preceded him. They had used the privilege only nine times in more than four decades.

The feelings against Jackson reached their peak during the 1832 reelection campaign. The Bank of the United States was the institution involved. A private company, the bank was, in effect, run by the American government. Clay and Webster were both attorneys for the bank. The government had withdrawn the bank's charter and both Clay and Webster fought to have it reinstated. Jackson opposed this and exercised his veto power.

The country understood that Jackson represented a strong federal government. The people liked what Jackson was doing and stood behind him. It was this strength on Jackson's part, as much as anything else, that helped him to be reelected in 1832. The election of 1832 was the first time in American history that a presidential candidate was nominated at a convention.

During Jackson's second term Indian affairs once more became an important issue. The Indian Removal Act had been passed by Congress in 1830. This forced Indians to allow themselves to be relocated by the government. Having been raised on the frontier and having fought against Indians, Jackson was not a strong supporter of Indian rights. He went along with relocation, because he believed that the majority of the American people thought it was right. He also justified this stand by arguing that it was what the Indians themselves wanted.

After Jackson left office the Cherokees were driven from their land in 1838. This forced march was known as the "Trail of Tears." Many Indians became sick and died. Although Jackson was no longer president, many people felt that the march was a result of Jackson's earlier decisions.

Jackson's bank policies also caused a financial depression after he left office. In 1837, the country began to experience hard times. But the country blamed them on Jackson's successor, Martin Van Buren.

President Jackson receiving delegates

Andrew Jackson on his way to Washington.

Life at the White House

During Jackson's two terms, some $50,000 in 1830s money was spent on improvements to the White House. Much of the money was spent on needed repairs and refurbishing. But some of it went in an effort to rid the mansion of any traces of John Quincy Adams and his family's lifestyle.

While Jackson lived in the president's house it was modernized. He wanted the original design by architect James Hoban be carried out. Hoban's plan had included an elaborate north portico at the front entrance of the White House.

On the inside, gaslight replaced oil lamps. And running water was added in 1835 to the presidential mansion. This meant that baths—and even a primitive kind of shower—were now part of an easier way of living at the White House.

While Jackson was in office the staff began work on the East Room. Although the room had been completed, it had never been properly furnished. Jackson oversaw the purchase of fine period furniture, luxurious carpets and a gilt chandelier. During his administration new china, cutlery and glassware for sumptuous dining entertainment were also bought. Although Jackson seemed to be a man of simple tastes, during his White House years elegant fish, duck and partridge dishes were frequently served, and fine wines flowed freely.

Jackson's inaugural celebration had been a free-for-all. But Jackson still had not learned his lesson. Even after the inauguration, he often held open houses at the White House. On occasions throughout the year people could come in off the street. Jackson opened the White House to the public on New Year's Day, the Fourth of July and on the anniversary of the Battle of New Orleans. Jackson thought of the White House not as his home but as "the People's House."

In 1835 the New York State Dairy Farmers sent a huge wheel of cheddar cheese to Jackson. It was not just a simple piece of cheese. It was two feet thick and four feet in diameter. It weighed an impressive 1,400 pounds. On Washington's Birthday in 1837, Jackson decided to open the White House for all to sample the cheese. There was such a stampede that the cheese was gone within two hours. And it left behind a mess and a lingering odor of cheese that took several years to get rid of.

There were changes made to the White House grounds as well. The well-known Jackson magnolias were planted in memory of Rachel Jackson. They now stand almost as tall as the White House itself.

Because Jackson did not have his beloved Rachel to stand by his side and serve as first lady, he had to rely on stand-ins to perform the official duties as hostess at the White House. Fortunately he had relatives at hand who were able to supply the need.

Jackson's wife's nephew, Andrew Jackson Donelson, served as his private secretary. Jackson's first "granddaughter," named after Rachel Jackson, was born in the White House. She became the apple of her grandfather's eye. Young Rachel was soon joined by two other children born to Emily and A. J. Donelson.

Emily Donelson was a lovely and slender woman with dark hair and a graceful neck. She was known for her social skills and tact. Although Jackson thought of Emily and Andrew Donelson's children as his own grandchildren, they were in reality his dead wife's grandnieces and grandnephews.

While his niece Emily served as White House hostess for most of Jackson's White House stay, another slight scandal was attached to Jackson's White House years. Peggy O'Neale Eaton was the wife of Andrew Jackson's secretary of war, John Henry Eaton. Although Jackson and his family liked her, most of Washington did not. Her first husband's death may have been a suicide because of his wife's infidelity.

When frail Emily became unwell, Jackson wanted Peggy Eaton to replace Emily as White House hostess. But Emily would not allow this and refused to let Peggy have the job. Much of Washington stood against Peggy Eaton. Jackson endorsed and supported her, in the same way he had stood beside Rachel. The incident gave rise to much gossip.

Andrew Jackson's cabinet passing judgment on Peggy Eaton's virtue.

Jackson's adopted son, Andrew Jackson, Jr., and his wife had three children of their own. At Christmas 1835 President Jackson and his family asked many Washington children to join them in festivities at the White House.

At four o'clock on Christmas Day the group gathered in the East Room to celebrate the holiday. The president joined in the festivities. But whether or not he threw any of the artificial snowballs provided has not passed down to us. Because of the mild winter, there was no real snow. The servants had made snowballs of starched cotton. There were plenty of Christmas decorations and food for everyone.

On another Christmas, the children warned their old "uncle" that Santa would not forget him. In the middle of the night they sneaked into his bedroom and filled a stocking for the aging president. In the morning he was delighted to realize he had been remembered. Even though Jackson's wife had died, there were still happy White House memories.

After the Presidency

After his two terms in office, Andrew Jackson left Washington and returned to the Hermitage in Nashville. And he seldom left it again.

The Hermitage, home of Andrew Jackson in Nashville

Famous painting of Andrew Jackson, by A. Durand

The Jacksons' first home on the property had been a two-room blockhouse. But in 1819 they decided to build a larger home. Although it was not enormous, it had good proportions and seemed like a much larger home. Jackson loved horses and raised them in the stables on the Hermitage gardens.

Jackson and Rachel loved the house and its beautiful grounds. The front lawn was shaped like a guitar—Rachel's favorite musical instrument. Although the brick house burned virtually to the ground in 1834, Jackson had the house rebuilt and restored almost to its original condition.

In his retirement at the Hermitage, the former president had time to spend with his family and time to reflect. Jackson's last years were troubled, but his popularity did not suffer. Mothers continued to name their sons after one of the country's most beloved presidents.

In 1838 Jackson finally yielded to a request that Rachel had made many years before. He became a practicing Christian and joined the local Presbyterian church.

Jackson was fond of having his portrait painted. He was also one of the first presidents to be photographed. In old age, portraits show him gaunt and drawn. Some of the gauntness, especially around the mouth, was due to the fact that Andrew's teeth fell out, one by one. He did own dentures, but he may not have worn them much. Loneliness and care also helped give Jackson a drawn and worried look.

A photograph of Andrew Jackson as an old man.

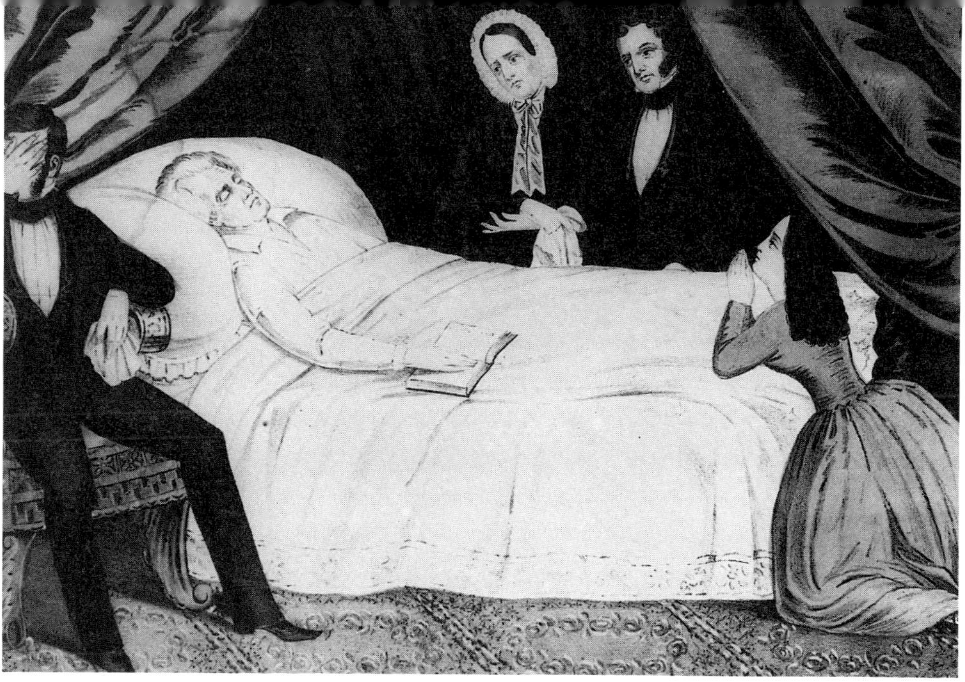

Andrew Jackson on his deathbed at the Hermitage.

A great deal of time and money in Jackson's final years went to paying off the debts of Andrew Jackson, Jr. who frequently got into debt. At one point his adoptive father was forced to sell the Hermitage to the state of Tennessee in order to raise money to bail Andrew, Jr., out. Today the house is run by the Ladies' Hermitage Association. It is open to the public year-round.

It was at the Hermitage on June 8, 1845, that Jackson died. He was 78 years old and had been suffering from symptoms of tuberculosis and dropsy. But it was probably a heart attack that killed him. His bedroom has been left exactly as it was on the day that he died. The former president was buried on the property next to his beloved Rachel.

The Face on the $20 Bill

Jackson left a political legacy that has made the U.S. presidency the most powerful governmental office in the world. He fought to expand presidential powers. He used the veto to exert strong control over Congress. In January 1835 the national debt was paid off. It was possibly the first and last time that the United States did not owe anything to anybody.

During his terms as president, the nation became industrialized. The Industrial Revolution that had begun in England was beginning to change the face of America. A host of new inventions were transforming the age-old methods of agriculture. And new machines meant that manufactured goods could be made cheaply and quickly.

On the negative side, however, Jackson was responsible for legislation that led to Indian removal and the Trail of Tears, during which thousands of Native Americans died. Jackson's name is also linked with the "spoils" system and charges of political favoritism.

Andrew Jackson was the first president who appeared to many to be an ordinary American. His origins were humble, which may have helped him capture the hearts of the American public. His popularity never waned, and some felt he was even more beloved and respected at the end of his presidency than he was at the beginning—something of a rarity.

Jackson was a planter, lawyer, judge, military commander and statesman. He balanced a military career with a career in politics at both the local and national levels. He was a man of contradictions: a man of great sense but little formal education; a military leader of determination but possessing no particular ability to devise strategy or command.

Jackson was the first self-made man who became president. And he inspired the feeling that almost any American could become president. Where some Americans had found George Washington aloof, they found Jackson warm and winning. In many ways he was just like most Americans. A lot of people feel that Jackson was the most popular president between Washington and Lincoln.

Jackson was honest, hardworking and forthright. He was the kind of man who has come to symbolize America. Even though his parents had been born abroad, he did not look to the traditions of the past or to the legacy of Britain or Europe. He was a man forged by America's frontier, a man who looked to the future for himself, his family and his nation.

The Jackson Monument at Jackson Square in New Orleans

For Further Reading

Anthony, Carl Sferrazza. *First Ladies: The Saga of the Presidents' Wives and Their Power, 1789–1961.* New York: William Morrow and Company, Inc., 1990.

Fisher, Leonard Everett. *The White House.* New York: Holiday House, 1989.

Friedel, Frank. *The Presidents of the United States of America.* Revised edition. Washington, D.C.: The White House Historical Association, 1989.

Klapthor, Margaret Brown. *The First Ladies.* Revised edition. Washington, D.C.: The White House Historical Association, 1989.

Lindsay, Rae. *The Presidents' First Ladies.* New York: Franklin Watts, 1989.

The Living White House. Revised edition. Washington, D.C.: The White House Historical Association, 1987.

St. George, Judith. *The White House: Cornerstone of a Nation.* New York: G. P. Putnam's Sons, 1990.

Stefoff, Rebecca. *Andrew Jackson, 7th President of the United States.* Ada, Okla.: Garrett Educational Corporation, 1988.

Viola, Herman J. *Andrew Jackson.* New York: Chelsea House, 1986.

The White House. Washington, D.C.: The White House Historical Association, 1987.

Index